AF450001

Anguish Impersonation

untold words get wings

antara

Writer's Pocket

First published by Writer's Pocket in 2024

email:publish@writerspocket.com

ISBN-13: 978-93-6083-803-4

www.writerspocket.com

To all who hold my hand in the depths of darkness,
Who watch over me when I lose myself,
To all, I will forever be thankful,
for never questioning the essence of my being.

The voices in my head, the emotions in my heart, are getting their names, are getting new words!

Contents

Acknowledgments

It is a memoir of the darkness I've
witnessed and am still enduring this
ceaseless night.
I am grateful for all of these and am trying
to keep documentation of them, marking
the blackboard with chalks of memory.
These pages are all crumbled, and it is
grueling to write a good story on them, but
I am still finding my way to make way to
compose jingles in them.
Because in the end,
'Rays of hope' are not always needed;
spending enough time in darkness will
make us adapt to it.
My second composition, in contrast to the
previous one, welcomes you all with its
scarred open hands to hug it and give it
your ardor!

About the Book

This book is an opener of many resentments I've bottled up since I've come to my senses. Throughout my life, in childhood, in school, and in later life, I've faced many miseries that I think I don't deserve. I've also encountered so many losses that declaring myself a 'loser' won't be enough!

I lose every moment, every day, every month, and every year. Even then, one thing I don't lose is my hope! I have high hopes for myself and the Almighty.

And here, my story takes a turn for the better! By the grace of the universe, I am living the happiest life I can ever have! It is all scripted. I am; we are all just actors here!

This book is one of the proofs of the miseries that broke me so badly, which in turn also helped me be the person I am today! This book is a milestone in my suffering and is just the beginning!

In this trophy of my life, I welcome you all to be a part of it and share a life with me!

Tears fall like rain,
Cleansing, washing away the pain,
Sorrow leaving behind a sense of clarity

Sadness is necessary for our growth
Sadness is necessary; it is part of the ride
a reminder to cherish and to never divide
the beauty of the pain, the love of the loss
in the balance, we find our greatest gloss.

Micro Poems

I'm hearing, not listening
I'm listening not understanding
Even when I'm understanding,
I'm not caring
No words are making me a loving person.

I feel the need for a figure
who will save me from the storm;
who will put me on the ground.

Designs in the dark
Glowing like flesh
Sanity of red
Nowhere to be found.

My mindless mind
Surfing through the sea
With enormous waves
To be mindful again!

Time is flowing away, right?
Mine is paused
at the same place
Where in the dark light stops.

The pond with no wave
It's still like a picture from the book
Even a whirlpool can't move it now.

A sorrow, hitting so hard
Days paused, months stopped, and eyes were
closed
Only breaths prove I'm alive!

"Life is so good!"
"No, it's a 'no'",
It's only good for those people,
Who knows how to let things go!

A tightrope walk of emotions,
We strive for equilibrium
Between joy and sorrow,
And the highs and lows of the heart.

"You're a pessimist," you shouted
The hallway heard you with me
when you make me the one!

Oh, it will only be me
So what? Let it be only me
Who cares? It's only me.

Enough of black and grey
Enough of the shades that don't stay
It is the night, not the day.

Where the road ends and the horizon calls,
That's where our hearts find their true walls.

In this darkened room, where shadows play
I search for solace—a glimmer of light in the day
But like a mirage, it vanishes from sight
Leaving me lost in this endless fight.

Mistakes are bridges to the unknown,
Cross them with courage and make them your
own.

I see my home in my dreams every night
I see my home talking to me when all is quiet
I see that my home is the same as when I left it
I see the home that's waiting for me,
Like, it won't go anywhere without my permit!

Oh, how I yearn to leave the pain,
To find solace in love and peace again.
But like a ghost, addiction haunts me still,
A constant reminder of my greatest illness.

My soul is bruised, my heart is worn,
My will is broken, and my life is forlorn.
But still, I dream of freedom's call,
To rise above the chains that enthrall.

23

I stumble through each day with a frown
Feeling silly, feeling down
I can't remember things; it's such a bore
I feel like I'm stuck in a never-ending roar.

My mind is clouded, and my thoughts are hazy
I feel so dumb, I can't seem to see
The world around me is all a blur
I'm lost in thought; my mind is a churn.

In this game, the game of life,
Where I'm making my play
Finding myself on the losing way
All dreams and hopes,
They are fading away.

I feel nothing, yet I'm alive,
A ghostly presence, barely thriving.
The wind whispers secrets in my ear,
But they're lost in the void, without fear.

The weight of duty is heavy on my mind,
I find excuses and time to unwind.
But as the hours slip away, I see
The consequences of my laxity.

The world outside is cold and gray,
Where people pass each other by the day,
With eyes that see but do not see,
And hearts that feel but do not be.

29

I bought a pair of shoes
Ugliest one of its kind
I thought it'd make a difference
But no, it's the same, just like my mind.

Only time will tell; only time will show.
If they will learn to love and let go,
Or if they will remain as they are,
A people lost in callousness and scars.

31

Fly me above the altitude.
From where I can never find
The room I had to leave once
Not knowing the reason!

I've lost my way, and I've lost my drive.
I've lost the will to survive
The world moves on; it leaves me behind.
And I'm left to mourn, to grieve, and to find!

In the storm, I've lost your hand
Where I used to harbor my heart strongly.

A car is honking at my door
The monster must come out.
In the shape of a human
It only sucks soul!

35

Too little, too afraid, too insecure with a too-
truth
Simple is not as simple as I think it is!

Sleep is a friend of mine
But the fair-weather one!

I'm creating our empire
On the sand with my hands,
Only to be washed away by the tides.

When the mind is darker than the sky
The cloud is over the top;
Rain is needed, with a storm
To make it again, blue, clear, and fine!

Morning hair is a mess
the mirror's reflection laughs at me loudly
surviving as a hopeless fool.

I'm not sad; I was not that sad at all.
But why is the sky filled with persistent green
clouds?
Why is gloom dawdling over the mind?
Why am I going on the route I never entered?

Oh, the ache that pierces deep and true,
when feelings start to fade anew.
For in their absence, I am left to face,
the reality of a love that's lost its place.

The walls of fear close in tight
A suffocating grip that holds with all its might
The screams are muffled by the chains of doubt
But still, they rise with a desperate, anguished
shout.

Free-Verse Poems

In stolen glances, I steal away,
Moments of tenderness in a world of gray,
The thrill of being together, yet apart
A love that's forbidden yet deep in my heart.

In the silence, I hear your name,
A whispered promise, a love that's not tamed,
It's a secret kept, a true heart
A love that's hidden yet forever shines through.

Shame in my mind
That I'll become weak
That I'll never be the same
That world will never see me the same
That things will never be the same.
That I am curling into a spiral coil
That is my fear.

That holds me, turns me, tortures me,
That I am in tears
All this is just an illusion
All this is just a thought.
All it takes is just an imagination
All is just here for a moment.
All will be gone
With a bit of sprinkled sauce over a piece of
onion!

I thought talking to you would change my day
It's Sunday, and maybe it'll brighten up with
your voice
No, it didn't
My thoughts and my assumptions are wrong,
Completely wrong!
All the black waves I am passing through
Hasn't changed with your words!
Changed? No, affected!
It didn't!

It used to, but not now!
Time's changed me, and so has your behavior
Nowadays, I don't call, nor do I say anything
I even don't ask your whereabouts!

It's 2024, and it has many new days left
This gives me more than a thousand options to
choose
To choose my feelings, my words
And I choose myself
Before you

No more frailty, overflowing of emotions
All I want is to preserve it for me
I won't tell you a word
But you'll know it eventually
Not by me, but through me.

"How cruel!" you'll think
But I only have it!
I want to live, and you know that.
I only have me; you don't know that.

To live, to grow, and to glorify my life
How little is left?
I can only dedicate these,
I dedicate my pages to you!

On cracked and worn surfaces, I see
An imperfect beauty is still shining free
A golden glow highlights the flaws
A radiance that whispers, "Beauty is not in law"!

In the imperfection, I find a strange allure
A humble beauty that still endures
So let me cherish the cracks and the flaws
The impermanence that makes beauty's laws!

Like a moth to the flame, I'm drawn to her fire,
A burning passion that my heart aspires to.
But with each kiss, I lose my desire,
To break free from her deadly, loving snare.

Oh, how I yearn to be set free,
To shatter chains that bind me to thee.
But still, I'm drawn to her sweet melody,
A haunting call that echoes in my memory.

Wild is wilder, even not the wildest
A storm is stormier than anything else.
I see them over the bridge
I see them from my outer side
I don't see them
I don't stay there
I will never sympathize
Because,
It's scary.
Because,
I'm scared.

I fear that I can never recover,
but is it really real
Is it that harmful?
I will never know
Because,
It's scary
Because,
I'm scared
To get there
To be there
To be there!

This is not the world I've ever dreamed of
This is not reality; I wanted to be real
My world cannot be like this,
This just does not fit with my sanity!

Oh, that must be a bad dream,
I must be sleeping
Who's going to tell me this is my dream?
I'm destined to; I'm forced to
Make my own reality!

I woke up in a dark room
Lights are closed by the sheet
I don't even know the time.

Oh, it's half past eight
Five minutes turn into fifteen
To recall where I was last night
Where did I leave that nightmare?
To slip into virtuality?

I was sleeping, and that was perfect
Why do I need to wake up?
I don't want to face the same
That I've left with lots of crumbs!

"It was better when I was sleeping."
The sigh in my mind never helped
It wants to escape, but there is no way I can find
I am going through this mess like I was
I can't escape my fate, no matter how many
times I want!

"It's not the end," I whispered to myself
"But it's harder today, and I can't fight back with
this."

53

You name it, and I'll say it.
I'll name all the things I've lost.
The list is endless.
For you, it's needless.
For me, that's all I have.
That's all I had, and that's all I lost.
That was me.
That was my identity!

55

If leaving my loved ones
for their better
Is this a nightmare for me?
It's the peace,
I have none.
To try, to cry, and to make a face wry
I have no one to hold me back.
I'm grateful not to have one!

Time stands still, yet my heart races fast
as the weight of being, settles like a heavy cast
I feel the gravity of every breath I take
the responsibility of life is like a fate I can't
escape

At this moment, I am searching for a reprieve
a respite from the weight, a chance to breathe
and leave
but like a shadow, it follows me still
the anxiety of existence is a constant, nagging
thrill!

A beautiful lie
Draped in silk and lace
Whispered with honeyed words
But harboring thorns beneath

It sparkles like diamonds,
But it holds no truth within
A mirage of perfection
That crumbles in the light

Yet we cling to its allure
A siren's song in the dark
Sometimes, the lie is more
More beautiful than the harsh reality.

It is burning like charcoal, heated, and lit in
bright red.
Small lumps of smoke, with a mixture of ashes
rising upward like a circle of hell
As it rises and blends in the air, the room is
warming up.
In the empty room, the grime of his body was
filled with his ashes.
Here live the touches of me with the voices of
him.

A bed, a muddy sheet, a yellow pillow, and a
broken chair
Yellow rays from the eastern window fill them
with sorrow.
Still, the light, I'm thankful for it,
At least when it comes to saying hello.

But in the southern part of the room, no
brightness can ever brighten it up.
Never will it see your face; you never know how
you cheered me up!

Every noon that's heated, hit the room, hit my
soul.
I'm patient with your patience,
My feet are burning like pieces of coal!

I'll revisit the wound, scathing upon it, and I'll
make it worse
A wound that was once nearly healed will be
made alive again
It'll bury me again in the unfathomable grief
I know that I need to open it soon.

Unless it'll create much more mess
It will eat my brain
Will cut me into pieces
It will give me away
It'll bury me again
This time forever
And I am not going to make this happen again.

To myself in late thirties,

Don't be sad, as I chose this path
I know you're bearing the consequences
I know it all
But you also know, maybe you've forgotten
It was all necessary
To connect me with you
I need to be selfish. I need you to think of me,
If not, I will be destroyed
Like that time, once again
I am choosing myself before anyone else
I am choosing to be with you!

Choosing one from two
It's not easy!
When one is strong as the other
Still, needs to choose one;
And with much thought
One is chosen.
And one is not!

Spotlight is on one
And not at the other
What about it?
No one looks at that.
Have our hawk eyes caught the second again?
No, the light is on the first

The second is also the leader,
Leader of the darkest queue
Larger than a meter
Where each second becomes a new!

My life is in your hands
It's just a breath away!
No, not the simple
The greater and deeper ones

"Close your eyes and take a deep breath."
They say
They said it right.
It's just a breath away.

It's not working, not working like it's supposed
to do
A lot of trials are trials only
They don't know how to go.

Don't you miss me?
Don't you want to see me?
Don't you want to take it back?
The last words you'd said to me?
Is it that easy?
Is it that fun?
To leave is to let go.
One moment all was there,
and the next there was none!

Is it that painful?
Can't you see me grow?
Time has paused since then.
Everything seemed too slow!

Can you hear my voice?
Every night that cries
It just wants you.

Can you wait a little longer?
I don't think you can.
You can't even stand a minute,
To see the pain I'd go through.

I thought you were selfish.
You only thought about you.
I never saw the pain in your eyes.
I never sought the mother in you!
I was the one.
Who wants you again and again?
Just to hold you once more
I never thought about how you'd stand.
Seeing your child go through snow!!

The more time passed,
The more rage grew
The moment I think about you

I only saw
A hopeless me, crying to hug you.
Touch you with bare hands
But as it's said, it was all good.
At least good for you!

The scars on my skin are now growing deeper
and deeper
They're shaping them, sculpting, and making a
new figure
That is similar to me
Yet not same
That seems like me, but not me.

No, I'm not insane!
I've paused for a long time, and since then
you've gone.
And now a new me is knocking on my head and
taking my eyes towards it
The sky is dark, but the moon is there.
Just like it used to be
When I walked home holding your finger!

Some things go.
They fly above a little more, and then
They never came back.
They go forever.

And back home that is left
Only left back
Holding the same memories of faded smiles!

Is this the face I wanted to see?
I wanted to be lit with the last rays of the sun.
Is this the eye I'd fallen for so badly?
I wanted to dive and never sink.
Is this the smile I used to look at from the back
seat of the bus?
Is this the man I wanted to meet once in my
early life?
Is this everything I've ever imagined?
Is this the reality I wanted to be real?

Shame on it, shame on me, and shame on the
existence of it!

Now that you're telling me the story,
The story of your joy, your win, your fun, and
your glory
I'm listening, all you wanted was one day.

Now when I'm listening, I'm coming to know
That feeling—the feeling of the difference
Between reading a story and being a character
in it!

Maybe I wasn't raised right.
I wasn't raised in the perfect way to be chosen,
or to choose the right!
Or maybe I'm wrong?
Why then?
Why do I feel all rights are wrong?

Why do I feel all the small things are not so
small,
And the big ones are not that big?
What should matter doesn't matter to me;
My head keeps a checklist of all things that are
not free!
All is covered with gray snow and not white,
Where it is supposed to be white, right?
Or maybe I'm wrong?

Why then?
Why do I think things have all the negatives on
one side?
Why do we all end up in the dark and not in the
light?
Maybe I'm the wrong one;
All the time, every time.

Faces blend within a meaningless crowd,
My voice was like a whisper, untold, unheard.
The weight of life is crushing like a cloud,
And I'm trapped, unable to move around.

Days blend like a never-ending sea,
And I'm drifting, lost in misery.
The pain of my life is a constant sigh,
I long for peace, but it's out of sight.

My plan is not to write
My plan is to make a pile
My plan is to create boundless strips
Of memories to keep me thrive.

My plan is to run away
My plan is to go to sleep and don't wake;
My plan includes all the fails
I went and will go through.

My plan is to live in Neverland.
Once I reach the gate,
Not to stop, not to wait
Not to give up on what's written in fate.

Just because you don't understand, will it make
everything go away?
Just because you don't understand, will I carry
all the emotion alone?
Not crying, not blabbering, and not even
stopping talking to you?

Just because you didn't feel right at the right
time,
Can you take a different path, go away for
months,
and then come back with a smile?
Just to pretend things never happened?

The wreckage you'd created, the silted lungs of
all,
and what do you think will happen when you
come,
ignored everything and said nothing at all?
The piles of ashes, burned hopes, desires, and
future plans are all ruined,
and you're saying you are not in the mood at
that time?

Is this all a joke for you?

You name it, and I will say it.
I'll name all the things I've lost.
The list is endless.
For you, it's needless.
For me, that's all I have.
That's all I had, and that's all I lost.
That was me.
That was my identity!

There is an unutterable amount of pain I'm
going through
And the fun part is that I can't share it with
anyone!
Nobody's here to hear my voice
Nobody was there to share my joys.

It feels like my chest will explode
With unnecessary thoughts of you
With uncanny similarities, I found them in those
places
Once I've planned to spend
Together with you.

Places are at their places
So are you and me
All the thoughts and plans are there
But the only missing thing is
Not becoming reality
Of all our plans!

You know I loved you, and I knew you do
But what happened on that day
It was rude, I was hurt, and you were ignorant,
deeply!

Your words pierced my heart,
Shook it to its bottom and core
Don't I even deserve an apology?
Was it so normal for you?

Did you just ignore it?

You contacted me, and calls and messages were
some
I was shaken enough to see your name
How can I even pick it up and

Tell you how I am!

Don't think I ever miss you,
You were on my breath
I miss you when it's hard for me
Cause I'll still love you
Even after I am caught by death!

My memories linger, a ghost of what we had
a lost love, like the lost leaves of last autumn
a faded beauty, like the glow that once shone
bright and slow
You let me fly away
into the vast sky, without a word to say
I searched the horizon for a glimpse of your face
but like the wind, you vanished, leaving only a
space!

They told me you found love,
A heart that beats for you alone,
They say it is real,
Found your heart's ideal,
A pure love, kind and true,
Love meant for me and you.

I hear these words:
I feel a pang of sorrow,
A heart that reveals the love we had,
The love we lost,
The memories still linger,
Like snowballs of frost.

With every stroke of the brush, I pour my soul,
Into a canvas that will soon grow old.
The colors blend, the beauty shines,
But as a sunset, it will fade with time.

The beauty I create will soon disappear.
I know the truth, yet I still strive,
To create, to love, and to live,
Though it won't last long.

In moments like these,
I find my peace,
A sense of purpose,
A world to cease.
I am reminded to cherish the process,
To find joy in the journey,
Not just progress,

For even in impermanence, there's beauty to
behold,
A beauty that will forever be worth the effort,
Though it grows old.

Haiku & Senryu

In the shadows of dead
Life is mourning not song of grief
But to enjoy life itself.

Wide eyes with wide desire
Is taking one step at a time
Not right time to fail.

Striving each day for success
Spiraling in the maze of life's journey
Wanting to find my purpose.

Leaves whisper with gentle touch
Branches reach for the sky-high, but
Roots are holding secrets deep.

Spring stepped with vibrant thrill
Tulips are dancing with sunlight
Silence changed into a melody.

Sunsets are not yellow now
Pink, orange, and many more it adds
It was all for me.

A pen, a notebook, words
Meaningless flow of curly ink on paper
Emotions never found their meaning.

Dry leaves, long trees, afternoon
Empty, lonely, long way to the home
My feet are all I have.

A toy car on my table
Was a gift now all is past
A toy car and you.

Ice cream, chocolate, flower sticks
Long talks, no talks, laughs into cries
Loves have lost their need.

Outlying gazes and lone hearts
all are lonely; busy in a crowd
Peace, nowhere to be found.

This calm flow of river
once wrecked hopes of many pebbles' lives
Shaming, making an innocent face.

93

My yearning with each breath,
Numbness flows through the heart and limbs.
I'm forming pieces of mold.

Musty scent lingers through room
It whispers memories of love and hate
Only walls know the truth.

Stream of tears in dark
Silent sobs, silent sufferings, holding the lost
The moon holds my pain.

Never-ending vision, losing the sight,
I fear to return to my land.
Of infinite expanse and vastness.

What'd you call that feeling?
That wants to shout its lungs out
But stops for unknown reasons?

Efforts of day and night
Putting it all in the burning pyre
Ghosting through essence of life.

Echoes of you softly call.
Echoing in the wind, you touch
Teaching how to live a dead life.

Busy streets, soaking in rain
Umbrella above me is of no use
All is dry inside me.

Dinner is placed for all
Seven seats, seven plates—all are empty
Only I am present there.

Last train is also passed
I am looking for since the morning
But no trace of you.

A sigh of warm breath
It's coming forcefully out of me
A hint of wildfire inside.

Two autumns with two shades
One is with the warmth of you
Another is a shade of vermilion.

105

Golden leaves are falling
twirling and fluttering on the ground
Filled with the summer's fleeting sigh.

Hidden beneath a calm surface
a churning whirlpool is waiting to burst
Just a matter of twinging.

Still air bears lingering echo
eerie wind is casting a widespread shadow
we carry past within us.

Light fading, all turning dark
Silent evening chilling, oozing the spark,
little hoping hearts returning home.

Hands that held tight one-day
are losing grip, are full of wrinkles
it's our time to nurture.

It's hard to write and cross all the fire ways I've
gone through.
Once again, just to make it a walk
Worth memorable, worthy enough to
Kaleidoscope of dismay washing away the pain
and sorrow
Sense for even a hundred years to go.

But the difference is in experience; as they say,
The difference is in the way I am;
We are all different.

That day was in the past, and I am just traveling
through it.
Going to a screening of a show
Once, I was the hero of it.

Aching from the same wound feels like an
unnecessary dig.
But to make a monument,
I had to cut open the steps once I was buried!
Now the fire doesn't burn, nor do I get chills.

I am acting again, just like in the past,
It's just for the show!
As the clock ticks, all sayings come true.
This time is hell;
It will not be the same once I pass it through!

About the Author

I have been a loner since birth; nature is my best friend. I am living, and I am the most grateful for that! I am a toy in the hands of the universe, living through words, making up stories, and giving them reality. That's how I live, and that's how I try to be a better human!

Have you written a book?
Publish it for free today!

Writer's Pocket is a publication house based in Vadodara, Gujarat. Established in 2016, we have a community of over 50,000 writers whose works we have published.

To publish your book with us for free, scan this QR code:

You can also reach out to us at:

Phone number: (+91) 8200 377 328
Email address: editor@writerspocket.com